# Tall Tilly

First published 2004
Evans Brothers Limited
2A Portman Mansions
Chiltern St
London W1U 6NR

Text copyright © Evans Brothers Ltd 2004
© in the illustrations Tim Archbold 2004
Reprinted 2005

British Library Cataloguing in Publication Data
Powell, Jillian
    Tall Tilly. - (Zig zags)
    1. Tall people - Juvenile fiction
    2. Children's Stories
    I. Title
    823. 9'14 [J]

ISBN 0237527944

Printed in China by WKT Company Limited

Series Editor: Louise John
Design: Robert Walster
Production: Jenny Mulvanny
Series Consultant: Gill Matthews

# ZIG ZAG

# Tall Tilly

by Jillian Powell

illustrated by Tim Archbold

Evans

Tilly was growing taller
every day.

She was taller than
all her friends.

She was the tallest girl
in her class.

She was too tall for
her clothes.

She was too tall for her bed.

She was too tall for the bath.

She was even too tall for Ben,
the boy she liked in class!

Worst of all, Tilly wanted
to be a ballerina.

But she was too tall.

Tilly hated it.

She wanted to be small
and dainty, like her
best friend, Molly.

Then Tilly's teacher had an idea.

She made Tilly Sports Captain.

Tilly was so tall that she scored lots of goals for the basketball team...

...and she saved lots of goals
for the football team.

She was so tall she won
every running race.

She jumped the highest
high jumps.

She jumped the longest
long jumps.

Everyone cheered for her.

# Tilly loved being tall after all!

Why not try reading another ZigZag book?

**Dinosaur Planet**       ISBN: 0 237 52667 0
by David Orme and Fabiano Fiorin

**Tall Tilly**       ISBN: 0 237 52668 9
by Jillian Powell and Tim Archbold

**Batty Betty's Spells**    ISBN: 0 237 52669 7
by Hilary Robinson and Belinda Worsley

**The Thirsty Moose**    ISBN: 0 237 52666 2
by David Orme and Mike Gordon

**The Clumsy Cow**    ISBN: 0 237 52656 5
by Julia Moffatt and Lisa Williams

**Open Wide!**       ISBN: 0 237 52657 3
by Julia Moffatt and Anni Axworthy